Always an Olivia

A Remarkable Family History

Carolivia Herron

Illustrated by Jeremy Tugeau

KAR-BEN
PUBLISHING

Kulanu be'chol lashon
For all of us in every tongue —C.H.

For Ruby and George —J.T.

My thanks in the preparation of this book go to the young readers and
critics of Tifereth Israel Congregation of Washington, DC: Marnie
Freeman, Laura Giron, Raphael Grimes, Elinor Mannon, Hannah
Mathis, and the Aleph Class. A special thanks also for my Kar-Ben
Editor, Jean Reynolds — you are a gift to me.

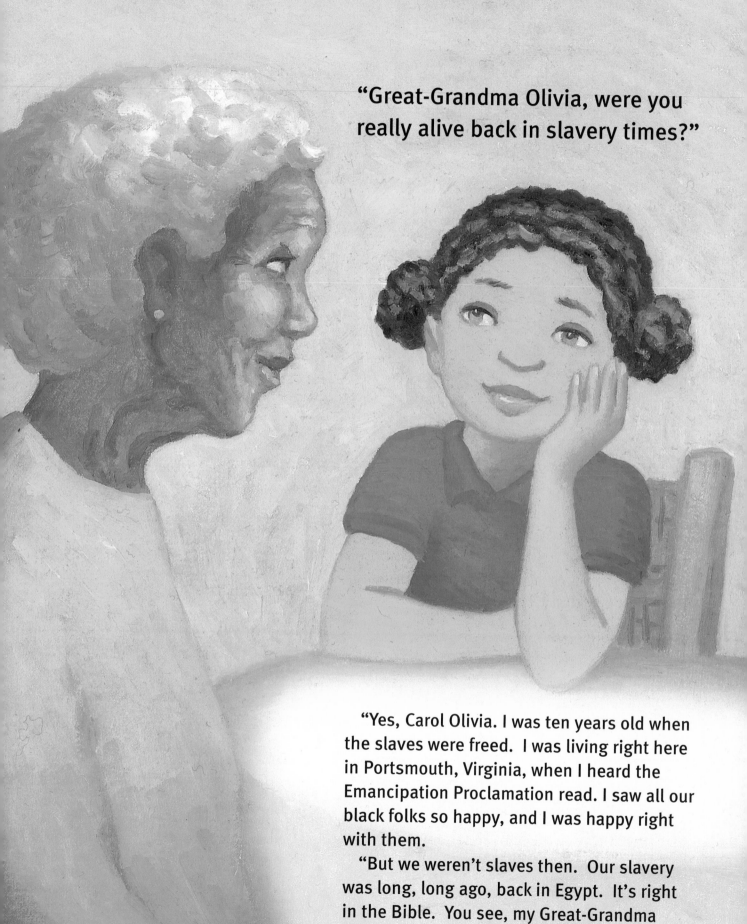

"Great-Grandma Olivia, were you really alive back in slavery times?"

"Yes, Carol Olivia. I was ten years old when the slaves were freed. I was living right here in Portsmouth, Virginia, when I heard the Emancipation Proclamation read. I saw all our black folks so happy, and I was happy right with them.

"But we weren't slaves then. Our slavery was long, long ago, back in Egypt. It's right in the Bible. You see, my Great-Grandma Sarah was a Jewish woman. She sailed the high seas to America."

Hundreds of years ago there was a Jewish family living in Spain near the sea. Spain was a dangerous place for Jews. And one day, someone stood in the street and said, "All Jews have to leave Spain right away, or the king's army will kill you." It was a terrible time.

The mother Naomi, the father Jacob, and their five
children gathered up a few possessions and ran down
to the ocean. They boarded a small boat in the middle
of the night and sailed off to Portugal.

In Portugal they lived in the village of Almansil, so Naomi and Jacob took the name Almansil as their family name. They gave up their Jewish name because they were afraid to be known as Jews.

The Almansil family loved Portugal. Benjamin, the oldest son, was a fisherman alongside his father. And Hannah, his sister, sold fish beside her mother in the market.

On holidays, the Almansil family loved to walk on the tall cliffs of Vale do Lobo and look at the ocean.

On Fridays, Naomi secretly made a special Shabbat bread called challah. Hannah went to the sea cliff and picked flowers for the Shabbat evening table. Her brother Benjamin brought home his best fish from the seashore. And every Friday their father brought Hannah and Benjamin small wooden toys he had carved while he was out on the sea waiting for the fish to bite.

They didn't want people to see them doing Jewish things, so Naomi closed the shutters tightly before she lit the Shabbat candles.

But the family's happiness in Portugal did not last. Just as in Spain, people began to persecute the Jews. Once again, the Almansils were forced to pack up their few possessions and leave quickly. This time they boarded a big ship with many other Portuguese Jews and sailed across the Mediterranean Sea past Spain and France, until they landed in Venice, Italy.

For many generations, the Almansil family lived
happily in Venice among other Jews who had escaped.
Life was good, but they never forgot Portugal.

In 1787 one of the descendants of Naomi and Jacob, Asher Almansil and his wife Miriam, had a daughter. They named her Sarah Shulamit. They sang a song of joy the first time they took her to the synagogue in Venice.

"Joyful, joyful are all who live in this house.
Joyful is the lovely daughter of our house.
Joyful are the mother and the father
of the child who dwells in this house!"

And Sarah Shulamit
really was full of joy. She
learned how to dance, and
she sang new songs.

Her father would take her for walks by the sea and tell her
the story of their ancestors who lived by the sea in Spain,
Portugal and Italy. She especially liked to hear about
Hannah, the Jewish girl who sold fish in the market and
loved to walk on the sea cliffs of Portugal.

One day, Sarah was walking by the sea wearing a dark head scarf, typical of those worn by Jewish women. A group of pirates recognized her as Jewish and kidnapped her for ransom. They imprisoned her in their pirate ship with other captured Jews. They planned to sail across the high seas to North Africa where they knew that wealthier Jews would pay them silver and gold to free their brothers and sisters.

Sarah never saw her family again.

All through the voyage, Sarah was terrified. Where was she going? Who would help her? She cried when she saw the evil pirate flag flapping in the breeze.

But all the time Sarah was crying, a man named James was watching her.

James had been kidnapped, too. The pirates had threatened to kill him if he would not join them. So James was pretending to be a pirate until he could escape.

When the pirate ship neared the city of Tripoli, Libya, James whispered to Sarah, "I'm going to help you. Don't worry."

Together, they came up with a plan. James tied Sarah's hands behind her back. He put a cloth over her mouth and tied a rope around her waist. When he was sure the captain was asleep in his cabin, James dragged a weeping Sarah off the ship.

"Where are you going?" one pirate demanded.

"I'm taking this woman to Zini, the rich Jew on the Alexandria Road. He will pay us a huge ransom for her. The captain told me to take her."

So the pirates let James and Sarah walk away.

As soon as they were out of sight, James cut the ropes from Sarah's hands and waist. He threw away the cloth that was over her mouth.

Sarah and James smiled at each other. It was good to be free.

The two of them decided to seek help at a synagogue. They waited until the men came for afternoon prayers. Sarah approached them and bowed her head. "*Sh'ma Israel, Adonai Eloheinu, Adonai ehad.* I am a Jew. Please help me, in the name of our God."

The men listened to Sarah's story. "Those pirates will be here tomorrow with the rest of their stolen Jews," the rabbi said. "If they discover you and James have escaped, they will kill you both. And if they find you here, they may harm our village."

"Sarah, you have to hide. James, I have an idea for you."

They walked up a hill and the rabbi pointed to some ships in the port.

"Those ships belong to the United States," the rabbi said. "James, you must go to the port, get on one of them, and sail to a new life in America. Here is some money to help you get away. And, Sarah, tonight is Shabbat. Here are candles to light when you get to your hiding place."

Sarah was very unhappy to have to leave James. And James did not want to leave Sarah. He whispered in her ear, asking her to meet him at the boat that evening. And Sarah said, "Yes."

When they got to the ship, the marine captain agreed to let them come aboard. And he also agreed to marry them! They sailed to the beautiful, peaceful Georgia Sea Islands off the coast of the United States where pirates wouldn't bother them anymore. The year was 1805.

After her wedding, Sarah began using her Hebrew middle name, Shulamit. It reminded her of her Jewish heritage. Shulamit means "peace," and she wanted peace after all of her family's wanderings on the high seas.

In Georgia, Sarah Shulamit and James lived with the Geechees, black people who had come from West Africa. They wove clothes and sang songs so beautiful that they enchanted the ocean tides. These Geechees were free, even though, at that time, other black people were slaves in the United States.

Sarah began using the middle name Olivia, instead of the Hebrew name Shulamit. Even in America, she was worried about people hurting her because she was Jewish. She chose Olivia because it made her think of an olive branch, the symbol of peace.

Sarah Olivia and James felt at home among the Geechees. They wore the Geechee clothes and sang their enchanting songs. And Sarah Olivia lit Shabbat candles like the ones the rabbi had given her in Tripoli.

James and Sarah Olivia's children married Geechees, as did their children's children. They earned their living catching and selling fish.

Sarah did not have a synagogue to go to on the Georgia Sea Islands. She forgot almost everything about being Jewish. But some things Sarah didn't forget.

She didn't forget her father Asher, and named her
son after him. In English he was known as Oscar.
And Sarah didn't forget that her middle name,
Shulamit, meant peace. She asked her children
to give one little girl in every generation a
name that meant peace.

And Sarah didn't forget to light the Shabbat
candles on Friday nights.

And Sarah's daughter didn't forget to light the
Shabbat candles on Friday nights.

And Sarah's daughter's daughter didn't forget to light
the Shabbat candles on Friday nights.

And Sarah's daughter's daughter's daughter is me . . .

"And so, Carol Olivia, that is our story. And I have been waiting all summer for you to visit me so I could tell you."

"That's such a good story, Great-Grandma Olivia. Is it really true?"

"Child, don't you know? It's absolutely true— well, mostly. At least all the important parts are true. There really was a Jewish man named Asher in Italy who had a daughter named Sarah who was stolen by pirates. And you know that your father's name is Oscar, which is another way of saying Asher. And you were named after my great-grandmother Sarah."

"What about my name, Great-Grandma? I thought I was named after you. Am I named after your great-grandmother Sarah too?"

"Yes! Both, child, both. In every generation a little girl is named Olivia. You are the Olivia of your generation. That's how we remember."

Jews and Racial Designation — An Historical Note

Jews were not considered white until the early twentieth century, and when in 1957 my great-grandmother told me this story of our Jewish ancestors, it was clear that she did not consider our Jewish forebears white. The concept of there being only three races (Asian, European, and African) is relatively recent in the history of racial designations. In the nineteenth century, there were hundreds of races, most, including Jews, being considered neither black nor white.

Perhaps these historical perceptions of race explain why, in 1805, the newly formed U.S. Marines settled my Jewish ancestor, Sarah Bat Asher, among the Geechees on the Georgia Sea Islands. Although the Geechees are descendants of West African slaves, on the island where Sarah and her ex-pirate husband made a home, the Geechees lived as free people—probably because the slave owners had died off through diseases and infections against which the African population had inherited medicinal antibodies. So to an early nineteenth-century U.S. Marine captain, it was reasonable to settle free Jews with other free nonwhite people—the Geechees of the Georgia Sea Islands.—*C.H.*

References:

Azoulay, Katya Gibel. *Black, Jewish, and Interracial: It's Not the Color of Your Skin but the Race of Your Kin, and Other Myths of Identity.* Durham, NC: Duke University Press, 1997.

Brodkin, Karen. *How Jews Became White Folks and What That Says about Race in America.* New Brunswick, NJ: Rutgers University Press, 1998.

Jacobson, Matthew Frye. *Whiteness of a Different Color: European Immigrants and the Alchemy of Race.* Cambridge, MA: Harvard University Press, 1998.

Roediger, David R. *Working Toward Whiteness: How America's Immigrants Became White.* New York: Basic Books, 2005.

Copyright © 2007 by Carolivia Herron

Art copyright © 2007 by Lerner Publishing Group, Inc.

Kar-Ben Publishing
A division of Lerner Publishing Group, Inc.
241 First Avenue North
Minneapolis, MN 55401 U.S.A.

Website address: www.karben.com

Library of Congress Cataloging-in-Publication Data
Herron, Carolivia.
  Always an Olivia : a remarkable family history / by Carolivia Herron ; illustrated by Jeremy Tugeau.
    p. cm.
  Includes bibliographical references.
  ISBN 978-0-8225-7049-3 (lib. bdg. : alk. paper) 1. Herron, Carolivia--Juvenile literature. 2. African American women authors--20th century--Biography--Juvenile literature. 3. Children's stories--Authorship--Juvenile literature. 4. Jewish women authors--United States--Juvenile literature. I. Tugeau, Jeremy. II. Title.
  PS3558.E7594Z46 2007
  813'.54--dc22   2006033680
[B]

Manufactured in the United States of America
1 2 3 4 5 6 – JR – 12 11 10 09 08 07